PIRATES IN PANAMA

Pirates in Panama

By F. N. Monjo

PICTURES BY WALLACE TRIPP

SIMON AND SCHUSTER, NEW YORK

Text copyright © 1970 by F. N. Monjo
Illustrations copyright © 1970 by Wallace Tripp
Published by Simon and Schuster, Children's Book Division
Rockefeller Center, 630 Fifth Avenue
New York, New York 10020

First Printing

SBN 671-65119-6 Trade
SBN 671-65118-8 Library
Library of Congress Catalog Card Number: 79-101891
Manufactured in the United States of America

JM749pi

For my wife

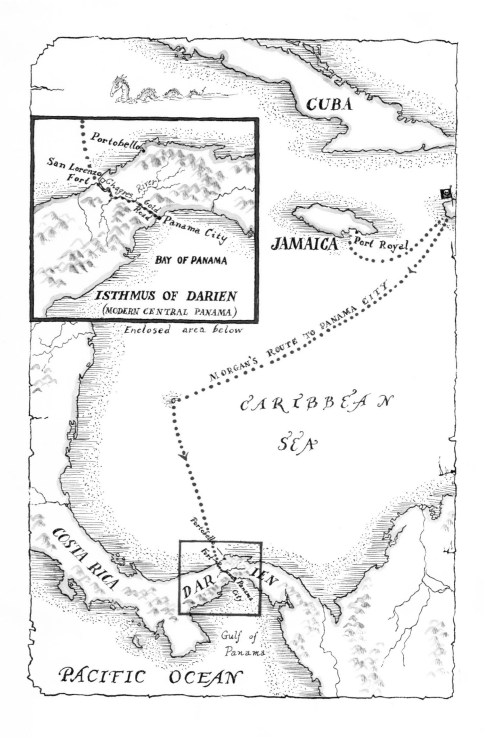

CUBA

Portobello

San Lorenzo
Fort

Chagres River

Gold Road

Panama City

BAY OF PANAMA

ISTHMUS OF DARIEN
(MODERN CENTRAL PANAMA)

Enclosed area below

JAMAICA

Port Royal

MORGAN'S ROUTE TO PANAMA CITY

CARIBBEAN
SEA

COSTA RICA

DARIEN

Portobello

Fort

Panama
City

Gulf of
Panama

PACIFIC OCEAN

The Altar of Gold

Brother John was the happiest man
in all Panama.
From the top of his church
he could see every house in town.

7

He loved everyone in Panama.
He loved Don Luis, the governor.

He loved stingy Don Pedro.

He loved silly Doña Margarita.

He loved his fat brown burro, Mariposa.

But most of all, Brother John
loved a little boy named Benito.

Benito had no mama and no papa.
Benito's mama and papa were dead.
"Brother John says Mama and Papa
are with the angels," said Benito.
And Mariposa the burro
shook her head yes, three times.
And the silver bells on her bridle
went "ching, ching, ting."

So Benito came to live
with Brother John.
Brother John taught Benito to read.
He taught him to fish
in the big round fountain in the garden.
He taught him to trim the grapevines.
He taught him to water the apricot trees.
Brother John taught Benito to pray with him
in church on Sunday
when all the people came.
And he taught him how to dust the altar.

13

"Mariposa," said Benito,
"Brother John wants our altar to be
the most beautiful altar
in the whole world."

And Mariposa shook her head yes,
three times.
And the bells on her bridle
went "ching, ting, ching."

"We will get two tall ladders, Benito,"
said Brother John.
"We will start at the top.
We will dust the angel.
Then we will dust
the picture of God the Father.
And we will dust all the statues,
one by one."

15

"Very well, Brother John," said Benito.
So they climbed the two tall ladders
to the top of the altar.
They dusted the angel.
They dusted the picture of God the Father.
And they dusted Saint Joseph.
And they dusted Saint Mary.
And they dusted the baby Jesus,
until everything on the altar
shone like a flame.
"It must be the most beautiful altar
in the whole world," said Benito,
when they were finished.
"Just look how it shines."
"Yes, it shines," said Brother John,
"because of all that gold."
"Gold?" said Benito. "Did you say *gold?*"
"Of course, Benito," said Brother John.
"Most of this altar is covered with gold.
Someday there will be nothing but gold,
pure gold, from top to bottom.
And everyone in Panama will call it
the altar of gold!"

Benito thought a moment.
"My mama and papa are in Heaven,
with the angels," he said.
"Is Heaven beautiful, like this altar,
Brother John?"
"No, Benito," said Brother John.
"Heaven is one hundred times
more beautiful than this altar of gold.
One hundred times more beautiful
for your mama and papa."
And so Benito loved the altar of gold more than ever,
because it was not as beautiful as Heaven.
"Brother John," said Benito,
"you are a poor man.
How is it that you can find
so much money for this altar of gold?"
"Come, I will show you,"
said Brother John.

19

And they climbed up on Mariposa the burro
and they rode into Panama.

Gold, Pearls, and Pirates

Brother John and Benito
rode to the house of stingy Don Pedro.
He was the richest man in Panama.
"Ah, Don Pedro," said Brother John.
"You will please give me
three pieces of gold."
"Three *more* pieces of gold, Brother John?"
said Don Pedro.

21

"For the altar, Don Pedro," said Brother John.
"Our altar is not finished yet.
But someday it must be covered everywhere,
covered, covered with gold.
We must have the most beautiful altar
in the whole world."

"I think already we must have
the most *golden* altar in the whole world,"
grumbled Don Pedro.
But he gave Brother John
three pieces of gold.

"So, that is the way it is
with the gold for the altar?" said Benito.
"That is the way," said Brother John.
And Mariposa the burro shook her head yes,
three times.
And the bells on her bridle
went "ching, ting, ching."

Next they rode to the house of
silly Doña Margarita.
"Ah, Doña Margarita," said Brother John,
"you will please give me
two big pearls."

23

"*More* pearls, Brother John?"
said Doña Margarita.
"Pearls for Saint Mary's crown,
on the altar," said Brother John.
"Ah, the altar!" said Doña Margarita,
and she gave Brother John
two big pink pearls.

Then they rode to the house of
Don Luis, the governor of Panama.
"Don Luis," said Brother John,
"here I am again."
"Brother John," said Don Luis,
"you have not chosen today to ask me
for more gold for the altar?"
"Yes. Gold for the altar," said Brother John.
"Someday our altar must be covered with gold.
From the angel to the floor.
From top to bottom. Everywhere, everywhere,
covered with gold."
"Covered with gold?" shouted Don Luis.

25

"Brother John, there will soon be
no gold left in all Panama!
It will all be stolen by the pirates!"
"Pirates?" said Brother John.
"Pirates?" said Benito.
"Pirates!" said Don Luis, governor of Panama.
"More than a thousand English pirates,
led by Henry Morgan."
"I have not heard of Henry Morgan,"
said Brother John.
"Ah," said Don Luis, "that is because
you think of nothing but your altar, Brother John.
Everybody else in Panama has heard
of Henry Morgan. He captured half my soldiers
and blew up the big stone fort at Chagres last week!
But Brother John did not hear of it!
I, Don Luis, sent a messenger to him,
and I said: 'Henry Morgan,
how did you capture my big stone fort in Chagres?
What marvelous new weapons did you use?'
And Henry Morgan sent back to me
the two pistols he wore in his belt.
'We used only ordinary pistols, Don Luis,'
said Henry Morgan. 'But we will cut our way

through the jungle. We will cross the mountains.
And we will show you how we *use* our pistols—
when we capture Panama!' "
"Henry Morgan sent you that message?"
said Brother John.
"Everyone in Panama has heard of it," said Don Luis.
"Everyone but Brother John."
"He must be one very bad pirate," said Benito.
"He is the very worst pirate of them all,"
said Don Luis. "Tomorrow
he will come down from the mountains.
I, Don Luis, and my soldiers
will try to stop him.
He will be in front of Panama
tomorrow afternoon."

27

"Then how can I save our altar, Don Luis?"
said Brother John.
"Save the altar?" cried Don Luis.
"Ah, Brother John!
How can I save Panama?"

&§ III ğ&

Something to Hide

Brother John and Benito
rode sadly away on Mariposa the burro.
"Can Henry Morgan the pirate
hurt my mama and papa?" said Benito.
"No, Benito," said Brother John.
"Mama and Papa are in Heaven
with the angels.
Henry Morgan cannot hurt them."

"Can Henry Morgan hurt our altar?" said Benito.
"That he *can* hurt," said Brother John.
"Unless we find a way to save it."

As they rode through Panama,
they saw men and women in the streets.
"Have you heard the news?"
they shouted.
"Hide your silver! Hide your gold!
Henry Morgan the pirate
is coming to Panama!"

Brother John and Benito
saw Don Pedro.
He was in his garden.
He stood beside his well.
He was dropping bags of gold and silver
into the water.
"Bring me my silver pitcher! My silver tray!
My silver spoons!" he called.
And Don Pedro threw them all down into the well
to save them from Henry Morgan the pirate.

Brother John and Benito
saw Doña Margarita.
She was in her garden, too.
"Bring me my rings! Bring me my beads!"
she called.
And she threw all her jewels
down into the well in her garden
to save them from Henry Morgan the pirate.

Brother John and Benito
rode back to the church.
They tied Mariposa
to a banana tree in the garden.
"You be a good burro," said Brother John.
"Do not eat the flowers.
Do not eat the green bananas
nor the apricots.
We must save our altar of gold from the pirates.
We have work to do!"
Mariposa shook her head yes, three times.
And the silver bells on her bridle
went "ting, ching, ching."

"How can we save our altar, Brother John?"
said Benito.
"It's too big to throw down the well."
"That's right, Benito," said Brother John.
"It is too big to throw down the well.
We must do something better.
We must have two big ladders.
And some buckets.
And two big paintbrushes.
And we must work all night long!"

First they hid all the statues.
Then Brother John and Benito
mixed a big batch of whitewash.
They placed their two ladders
on either side of the altar of gold.

Then they started high up, at the top.
They painted the angel with whitewash.
Then they whitewashed the top.
And they whitewashed the sides.
And they whitewashed the bottom.
They worked for hours and hours.
When morning came,
Brother John and Benito
had hidden every bit of gold
under a thick coat of whitewash . . .
except for six golden candlesticks.

Then they put away the ladders and the brushes.
But Brother John's and Benito's arms ached
so that they could move no more.

37

They were so tired
they sat down at the foot of the altar
and went to sleep.
Mariposa the burro waited quietly all night long,
under the banana tree.
She did not touch the apricots,
nor the green bananas.
And when morning came,
she fell fast asleep, too.

⊷§ IV §⊷

Henry Morgan the Pirate

Brother John and Benito
and Mariposa the burro
slept through most of the fighting.
They did not see Don Luis
march out of Panama with his army.
They did not see Henry Morgan
and his hungry pirates
charge down from the hills.

39

The pirates had had nothing to eat
for three days, for Don Luis
had stripped the country bare of food.
Don Luis thought he had a trick
that could stop the charging pirates.
He thought he could stop them
with a herd of angry bulls.
So Don Luis told his soldiers
to tie torches on the horns of the bulls.
When the torches were lit,
the soldiers drove the angry bulls
in among the charging pirates.
But Henry Morgan's men just laughed for joy!

They were so hungry they rounded up the bulls
and killed them.
Then they cut them up
and made a giant barbecue.
All the pirates then sat down
and ate their barbecued roast beef
right under Don Luis's nose.
And when they had finished eating,
they were readier than ever for battle.

But Brother John and Benito
slept through it all.

They did not hear the screams and the cannon.
They did not see the smoke and flame.

They did not wake when
Henry Morgan and his pirates
drove Don Luis and his soldiers
back into Panama.
They were still sleeping
when Don Luis called out to the townspeople:
"The battle is lost. But Henry Morgan
shall never have Panama!
We will burn the town!"
Brother John and Benito slept
while the people took torches
and set fire to their houses,
until all Panama was in flames.
They did not stir until Henry Morgan
tramped into the church.

"Wake up!" roared Henry Morgan the pirate.
"If this place were built of wood
you'd both have been fried to a crisp,
like bacon!"
The town was red with flames.
The air was thick with smoke.
Brother John and Benito rubbed their eyes.

"Bring everyone to me!" shouted Henry Morgan.
And his men dragged all the people of Panama
to him, in chains.
"Now tell me where you've hidden
your gold and silver," said Henry Morgan,
"or I'll slit your gizzards!"

There was stingy Don Pedro.
"Your gold and silver. . . ?" roared Henry Morgan.
Don Pedro's knees were quaking.
"In my garden, at the bottom of the well,"
murmured Don Pedro.
"Easy enough to fish it up again,"
said Henry Morgan.
So poor Don Pedro had to fish up
all the gold and silver he had thrown down his well.

47

Next came silly Doña Margarita.
She was almost too scared to speak.
"Your rings? Your pearls?" said Henry Morgan,
twisting the dagger in his belt.
"In my garden," whispered poor Doña Margarita,
"at the bottom of my well."
"A simple matter to fish them up again," said Henry Morgan.
So Doña Margarita had to fish up all her jewels
and give them to the pirate, with a sigh.
Everyone in Panama had to give Henry Morgan
everything he wanted,
until a huge pile of gold and jewels
lay heaped at his feet.

❧ V ❧

The Biggest Pirate in Panama

Then Henry Morgan turned to Brother John.
"Where is *your* gold, Brother John?" said Henry Morgan.
"Those six big candlesticks, are they gold?"
"They are," said Brother John.
"Take them. Take them all.
Take all the gold you can find."
"This altar . . ." said the pirate.
"How is it that there is so little gold

49

to be seen on this altar, Brother John?
And where are all the statues?"
"This altar is not finished . . ." said Brother John,
"though one day it will glitter with jewels and gold."
"Hmmm!" said Henry Morgan. "I will talk to the boy.
Benito, look me in the eye!
Where is the gold from the altar?"
Benito looked at Brother John.
He looked at the altar.
Then he looked at Henry Morgan.
Benito thought of his mama and papa in Heaven.
And he thought of Brother John's beautiful altar
as it used to be, shining like a flame.
Benito was afraid.
But he was not going to tell
Henry Morgan about the gold
no matter what happened.
Not even if Henry Morgan slit his gizzard.
"Where is the gold from the altar, Benito?"
growled Henry Morgan.

"Someday," Benito murmured,
"our altar will be covered with gold.
From the angel to the floor. From top to bottom.
Everywhere, everywhere, covered with gold."
"You see, Henry Morgan," said Brother John,
"the boy cannot tell you anything.
Besides, this altar is not *finished* . . ."
"And you have forgotten the bells
on Mariposa's bridle," said Benito to the pirate.
"The bells are solid silver. Do you want them?"
"Let the burro have her bells," said Henry Morgan.
"We have picked Panama clean of everything else.
Let's pack up our gold! Scoop up our pearls!
It's time for us to start for home!"

53

"Wait, Henry Morgan," said Brother John.
"You have taken our treasures.
We should have a favor from you in return."
"And what favor do you want, Brother John?"
said Henry Morgan.
"Ah," sighed Brother John,
"we need a bit of gold for our altar.
Today it is bare, as anyone can see.
But someday, this altar must be
covered with gold . . ."

"I know!" laughed Henry Morgan.
"From the angel to the floor.
From top to bottom.
Everywhere, everywhere, covered with gold.
Benito spoke of it, before.
How I wish I could see it now,
all covered with gold!"

"Well, Brother John,
how much gold do you want from me?"
"Let us say, ten thousand pieces," said Brother John.

"Ten thousand pieces," laughed Henry Morgan.
"But why shouldn't you have it, Brother John?
After all, I've taken everything else in Panama!"
And he threw Brother John his heaviest sack of gold.
Then Henry Morgan jumped on a horse
and hollered, "Get ready, me buckos!
We're leaving Panama. Ready, march!"
The pirates began tramping
out of the ruined town.

Brother John and Benito stood
next to Mariposa, by the banana tree.
Henry Morgan rode over to them.
He grinned at Brother John,
and he winked at Benito.

59

"Be sure to invite me back to Panama
when your altar of gold is finished!"
Then the pirate leaned down and whispered:
"You know, Brother John, nobody ever got
ten thousand pieces of gold from Henry Morgan before.
You're a bigger pirate than I am.
You're the biggest pirate in Panama!"
And Henry Morgan winked a second time at Benito.

And Mariposa the burro
nodded her head yes, three times.
And the bells on her bridle
went "ching, ting, ching!"

AFTERWORD

Almost everyone agrees that Henry Morgan left the island of Jamaica with an army of buccaneers, landed at Chagres and blew up the fort there, cut his way through the jungle, crossed the mountains of the isthmus, and captured the town of Panama in 1671. They agree that he and his men thoroughly plundered it, and that the new city was later built several miles away from where the old one had stood. People also agree that Henry Morgan returned from his raid so rich in gold and silver that King Charles II knighted him Sir Henry Morgan and made him governor of Jamaica.

But nobody agrees about much of anything else that happened that year in Panama. Some say that Henry Morgan was an honorable soldier; others say he was no better than a cruel pirate. Some say that the Altar of Gold was saved by Brother John, as this story relates; others say that that is only a legend.

Those who visit the Church of San José in Panama today can still see the Altar of Gold. The Augustinian friars there may repeat Brother John's story, for people in Panama have been talking of his deeds for centuries, chuckling over the way he saved the golden altar from the pirates—with a little whitewash, some quick thinking, and some love.

Nobody will ever know exactly what happened there in 1671; so I decided it would be permissible to add a little, here and there, in honor of Brother John. But for the most part I have told the story much the way they still tell it today in Panama, hoping it may be true.